I am a boy of color

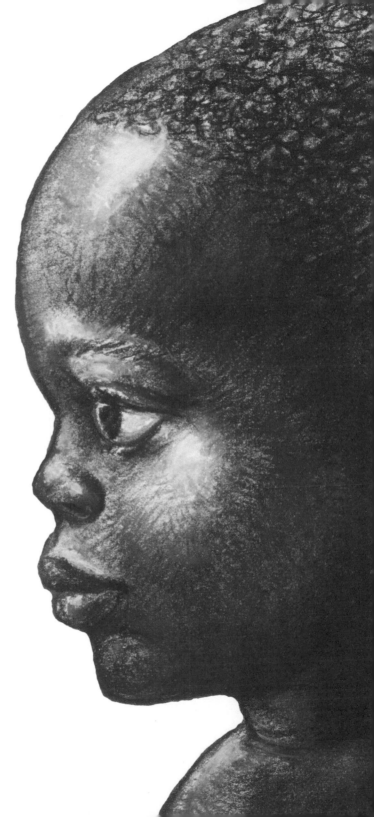

Written by Deanna Singh
Illustrated by Ammar Nsoroma

Presented by

www.storytotellbooks.com

A Project of

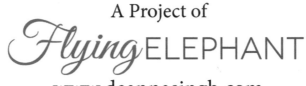

www.deannasingh.com

Published by Orange Hat Publishing
ISBN 978-1-943331-21-5
Third Edition

I Am a Boy of Color
Written by Deanna Singh
Illustrated by Ammar Nsoroma

www.orangehatpublishing.com

For Justin, Zephaniah, Zion and all the little boys of color that are making the world brighter!

When I look into a mirror, I see
CREATIVITY, an image of all that
could be.

When I look into a mirror, I see POSSIBILITY, the range of my ability.

When I look into a mirror, I see LOVE, for others and also for me.

When I look into a mirror, I see
HONOR, images of those who
came before.

11

When I look into a mirror, I see JOY, smiles, laughter, and giggles galore.

13

When I look into a mirror, I see INTELLIGENCE, a thirst for knowledge.

15

When I look into a mirror, I see

A REFLECTION OF GOD. I am his child.

What do you see when you look at me?

Please, see ME.

I am Unique.

I am Free.

I am Caring.

22

I am Proud.

23

I am Happy.

I am Smart.

I am a Boy of Color.

Draw an image of yourself!

CPSIA information can be obtained
at www.ICGtesting.com
Printed in the USA
LVHW072350270219
609025LV00003B/9/P